Flik
saves the day

Ladybird

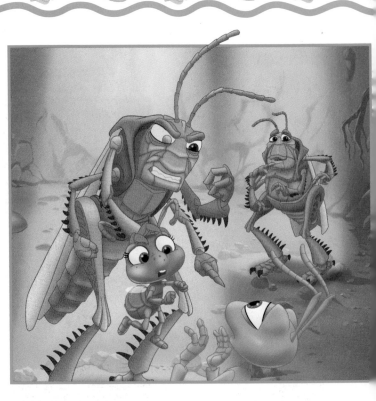

Princess Atta and the ant colony
were in big trouble. A gang of
grasshoppers was coming to
take all their food.

Flik set off to find some big bugs to help them. His little friend Dot came to say goodbye.

In the city, Flik met some bugs
who were fighting a gang of flies.
The bugs looked very brave.

Flik asked his new friends
to come and help the ant
colony, and they said yes.

The ants had a party for their new friends. They put on a play about fighting the grasshoppers.

"We're circus bugs, not heroes!"
whispered Rosie the spider. The
bugs decided to leave.

Flik ran after them. He begged his new friends to stay, even if they weren't heroes.

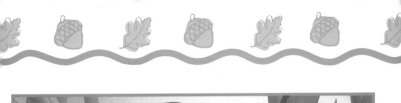

Suddenly Flik shouted, "Run!"
A big bird had spotted them!

9

Flik's friend Dot was floating
towards the bird on a dandelion
seed. She let go
just in time.

Francis the ladybird bravely
caught her. But they fell into a
crack in the river bed.

Heimlich and Slim helped by keeping the bird busy.

Rosie the spider
spun a silky net.
Flik and his
friends used it to
rescue Francis
and Dot.

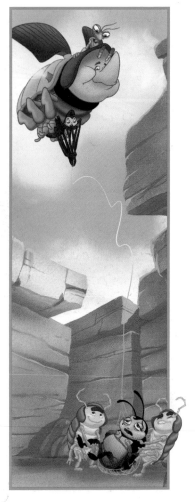

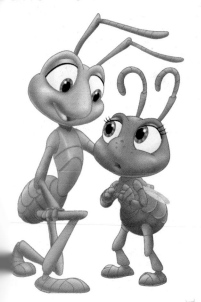

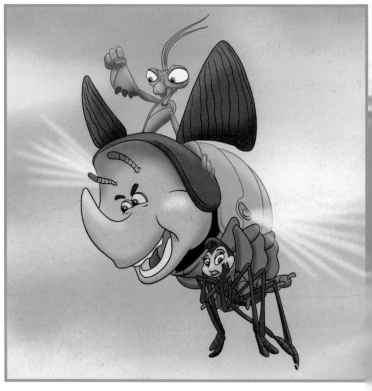

Dim the beetle flapped his wings
as fast as he could and quickly
carried the bugs to safety.

All the ants cheered for the brave bugs. Flik's new friends *were* heroes, after all!

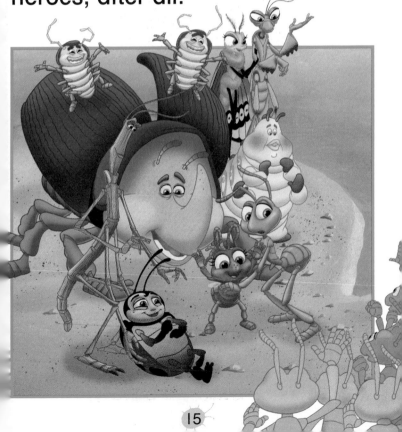